ANOTHER KIND

CAIT MAY & TREVOR BREAM

HARPER alley

An Imprint of HarperCollinsPublishers

WE KNOW
WHAT YOU ARE

SLIDE

CLICK

WELCOME, SIR.

4

GASP!

GOOD MORNING, SLEEPYHEAD!

GGRRMPH...

OW OW OW OW OW

flOP

14

PSST, SYLVIE--HOW COME CLARICE ALWAYS WORKS ALONE?

HOW SHOULD I KNOW?

SHE JUST GOT HERE AND SHE'S NOT SO FRIENDLY YET.

SHE'S SHY, I THINK.

I GUESS SO. I THINK **HER PARENTS DIED**... OR SOMETHING.

WHAT?!

WELL, I OVERHEARD THE AGENTS TALKING ABOUT IT...

THEY GOT STUCK IN A **BOAT NET** OR SOMETHING? I DON'T REMEMBER WHAT IT'S CALLED. THEY **DROWNED**.

SHE SAW THE WHOLE THING. GOT WASHED UP ON SHORE, GOT CAUGHT.

THEN THEY BROUGHT HER HERE.

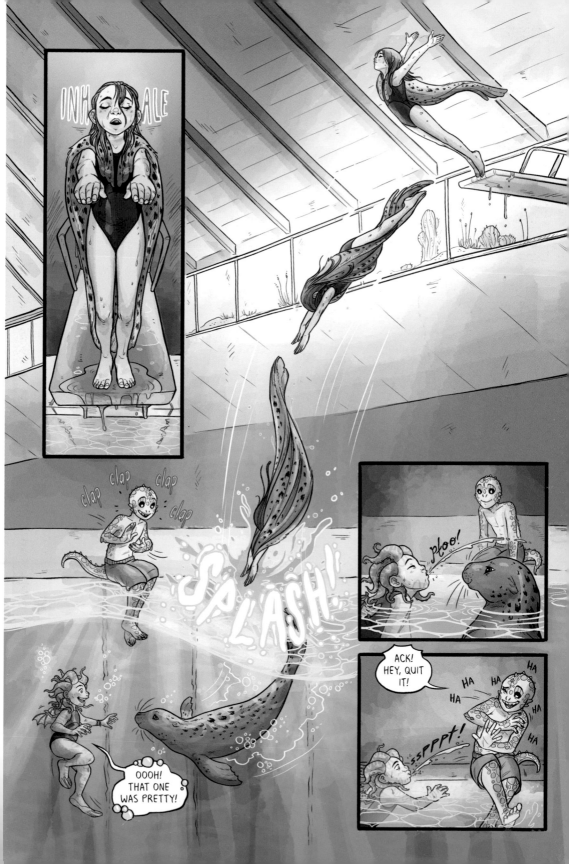

BLIP!

WHAAAAAAT DO YOU WANT, MAGGIE? I'M BUSY.

OH, UH, SORRY CLARICE.

WHAT'S WRONG?

WE KNOW WHAT YOU ARE

OMAR!! SOMEONE CAN **SEE** US!

SLAP!

WHAT?! SOMEONE IS TAKING PICTURES OF US WITH THE **WEBCAM**!

MAGGIE, GO GET AN AGENT, **NOW.**

O-OKAY!

SCAMPER

STAY CALM-- THEY'LL KNOW WHAT TO DO.

fwip

knock knock knock

SYLVIE, IT'S THE MIDDLE OF THE NIGHT.

YEAH, AND SINCE **THE BABIES** ARE ASLEEP, WE CAN ACTUALLY **TALK.**

YOU'RE STILL FREAKED OUT?

OF **COURSE** I AM!

HOW COULD SOMEONE HACK INTO THE COMPUTERS OF A SECRET GOVERNMENT FACILITY--

FROM THE OUTSIDE??

THIS PLACE IS COMPLETELY OFF THE GRID--

IT'S **SUPPOSED** TO BE SECURE. THEY TOLD US WE'D BE SAFE HERE!

CALM DOWN. IT COULD BE SOME IDIOT ON THEIR **LAPTOP** A THOUSAND MILES AWAY.

BUT WHAT IF IT ISN'T? **WHAT THEN?**

I DON'T KNOW. BUT RIGHT NOW THE AGENTS ARE PROTECTING US.

PROTECTING US?

THEY KEEP US LOCKED AWAY IN THIS **FANCY BOX,** THE SAME THING DAY AFTER DAY, AND EXPECT US TO SAY **THANK YOU SO MUCH,** MAY I HAVE SOME MORE CARDBOARD FOOD, PLEASE?!

BETTER LOCKED IN HERE THAN OUT WITH THE **NORMALS,** ISN'T IT?

NO.
NO, IT ISN'T. IF SOMEONE CAN HACK THE SYSTEM, WHO'S TO SAY THEY CAN'T HACK THE **LOCKS?**

33

CHAPTER TWO

YOU CAN RUN
BUT YOU CAN'T HIDE

MONDAY

TUESDAY

WEDNESDAY

THURSDAY

nudge

? ? ?

SHRUG

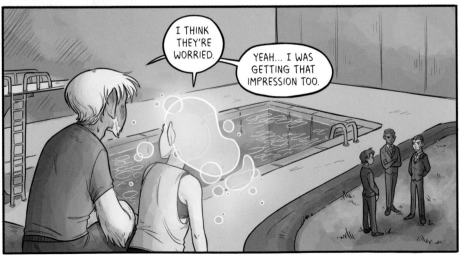

I THINK THEY'RE WORRIED.

YEAH... I WAS GETTING THAT IMPRESSION TOO.

SLAM!

BLOODY RIDICULOUS.

KEEPING US IN THE DARK...

WHISPERING BEHIND OUR BACKS LIKE THIS...

MAKING A FUSS...

fwip

RISE AND SHINE, GANG! BIG NEWS!

IT HAS BEEN DECIDED THAT DUE TO THE RECENT SECURITY BREACHES, YOU'RE BEING **RELOCATED** TODAY!

WE'RE **MOVING**??

YUP! AS SOON AS POSSIBLE.

CLICK!

GUHHHH...

THESE ARE FOR YOU TO PACK YOUR ESSENTIALS. YOU'LL NEED YOUR TOOTHBRUSHES AND AT LEAST ONE CHANGE OF CLOTHES. EVERYTHING ELSE WILL BE BROUGHT TO THE NEW FACILITY LATER.

WHERE EXACTLY ARE WE GOING?

THAT'S **CLASSIFIED**, NEWT. BUT REST ASSURED IT'S MORE SECURE THAN THIS FACILITY.

CLAP CLAP!

NOW, HOP TO IT!

LOOKS LIKE MAGGIE HAS THE RIGHT IDEA!

WHAT ARE YOU DOING?

DID YOU PACK YOUR TOOTHBRUSH?

GOTTA MAKE SURE ALL MY STUFFIES FIT!

OH... OOPS.

THAT'S OKAY, I'VE GOT IT HERE. YOU'RE PRETTY EXCITED, HUH?

YUP!! I'VE ONLY BEEN OUTSIDE **ONCE** BEFORE!

AND I DON'T REALLY REMEMBER IT... BUT I BET IT WAS **GREAT**!

DO YOU THINK THERE'LL BE **TREES** AT THE NEW PLAYROOM?

MAYBE WE CAN PLAY OUTSIDE THERE!

DO YOU THINK THERE'LL BE **OTHER KIDS** AT THE NEW PLACE?

MAYBE WE'LL GET OUR OWN ROOMS!

THIS ROOM SMELLS TOO MUCH LIKE LIZARD.

HEYYY!

sigh

YOU'VE ONLY BEEN HERE A MONTH AND WE'RE MOVING ALREADY, HUH?

zzziiip!

tuck

WELL... THE NEW PLACE WILL SURE BE BETTER THAN THIS ONE.

49

WHERE ARE YOU HEADING? I DIDN'T GET ANY ORDERS THAT WE WERE LEAVING THE ROAD.

I WAS BRIEFED RIGHT BEFORE WE LEFT. ADDITIONAL SECURITY MEASURE.

I THINK I WOULD HAVE HEARD SOMETHING ABOUT THIS.

IF YOU WEREN'T INFORMED, THEY MUST HAVE HAD A REASON TO **MISTRUST** YOU.

MISTRUST **ME??**

I'M NOT THE ONE TAKING A CAR FULL OF **CHILDREN** AWAY FROM THE SAFE ROAD--

THEY ARE **IRREGULARITIES**.

NOT CHILDREN.

NEWT. NEWT, YOU NEED TO WAKE UP.

RIGHT NOW.

HUH... WHA?

52

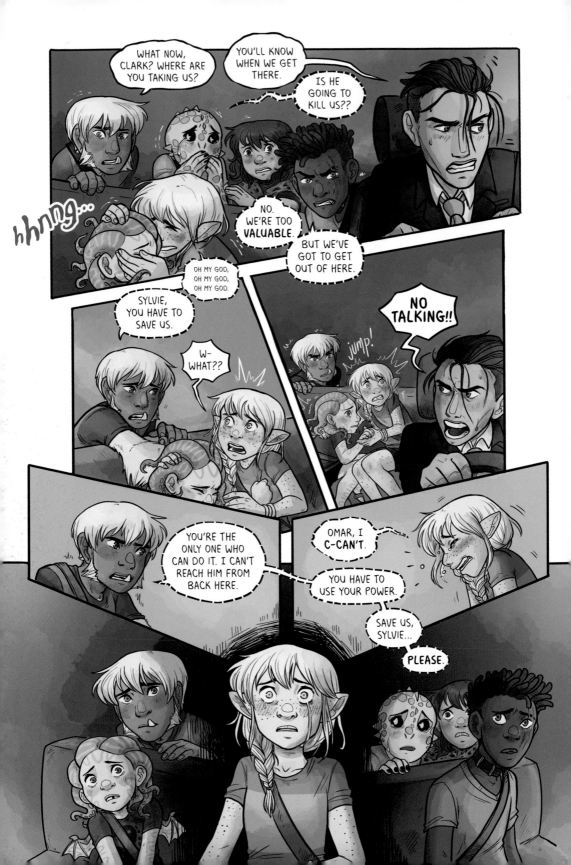

CHAPTER THREE

WHITEOUT

KA-KRASH!!!

NANI?? YOU OKAY?

I'M ALL RIGHT!

NANI... WHAT ARE WE GONNA DO?

WHAT?

WHAT ARE WE GONNA DO ABOUT ME?

WHAT IF I END UP LOOKING JUST LIKE DAD?

EVERY OUTSIDER IS AFRAID OF ME, AND IT'S JUST GOING TO GET WORSE!

THEY ALL THINK I'M A MONSTER, NANI.

ARE YOU?

W-WHAT??

ARE YOU A MONSTER?

I... I DON'T THINK SO??

IT CAN'T BE THAT SIMPLE!

YES, IT CAN.

IT'S UP TO YOU TO DETERMINE WHAT KIND OF PERSON YOU WANT TO BE.

THOSE WHO JUDGE YOU BY APPEARANCE, WITHOUT EVEN TAKING THE TIME TO KNOW YOU,

DON'T GET TO DECIDE YOU'RE A MONSTER.

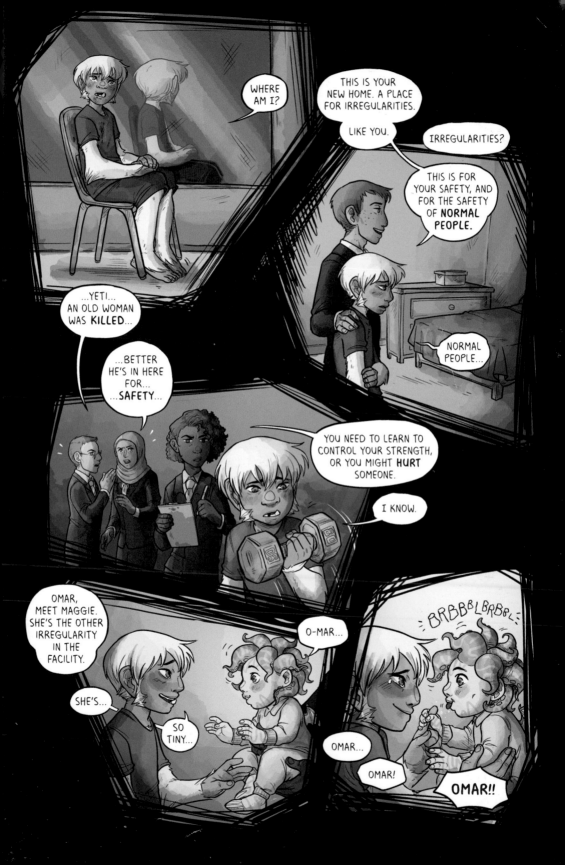

I'M GONNA TRY TO TALK TO HER.

OMAR?

HM?

...WHO IS **NANI**?

W-WHAT?

WHEN YOU WERE KNOCKED OUT, YOU KEPT SAYING NANI, NANI. WHO'S THAT?

NANI IS... A SHERPA WORD FOR **GRANDMA**.

OH, DID YOU HAVE A DREAM ABOUT YOUR GRANDMA?

WHERE IS SHE NOW?

IS SHE NICE?

SHE'S... SHE'S GONE, MAGGIE. A LONG TIME AGO.

OHH...

HEY, STAY HERE A MINUTE, ALL RIGHT?

WHY?

I NEED TO GO TALK TO SYLVIE. SHE'S BEEN THROUGH A LOT AND NEEDS HELP RIGHT NOW.

CAN I HELP TOO?

IN... IN A MINUTE, YEAH. I'LL BE RIGHT BACK.

OKAY.

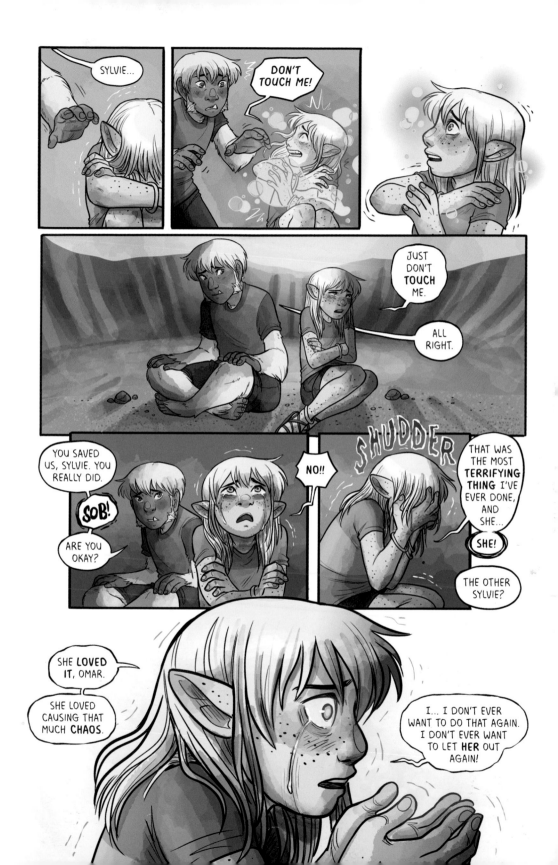

I THINK... YOU MIGHT **HAVE TO** SOMEDAY.

TCH! THAT'S RUBBISH ADVICE, THANKS A LOT!

I MEAN... ALL OF US HAVE **SOME** KIND OF **MONSTER** IN US, SYLVIE.

YOU'VE JUST GOT... A PARTICULARLY DIFFICULT ONE.

AND WE DON'T KNOW WHAT'S AHEAD OF US.

YOUR ABILITIES ARE **INCREDIBLE**, EVEN IF THEY'RE SCARY.

AND IF I'M BEING HONEST--

IF ANYONE CAN CONTROL A MONSTER LIKE THAT--

IT'S **YOU.**

YOU'RE THE SNARKIEST, SCARIEST, MOST BADASS PERSON I'VE EVER MET.

YOU IDIOT.

-SNIFF-

OF **COURSE** I AM.

BUT I'M NOT DOING THAT AGAIN ANY TIME SOON.

NOT UNTIL... NOT UNTIL I'M READY.

NEWT--COULD YOU GET OUR BAGS OUT OF THE TRUCK?

WE NEED TO FIGURE OUT WHERE WE'RE GOING AND WHAT WE'RE GONNA DO NOW.

HEY, TINY.

OH... UHH.

THE... UH... THE **AGENTS** ARE STILL IN THERE?

SHE... UHM. AND HE... THEY **WEREN'T MOVING**, WE THINK THEY MIGHT BE... DEAD. SO WE DIDN'T...

I'LL GET THEM.

OH! THANKS, JAALI.

ANYWAY...

I FOUND THIS!

IT'S AGENT RAMIREZ'S **SATELLITE PHONE**.

I THINK I CAN GET SOME KIND OF **INTERNET CONNECTION** WITH IT.

HOOK IT UP TO MY O-PAD AND TRY TO FIND A WAY **OUT** OF THIS **DESERT**!

GOOD THINKING!

HE TRIED TO KILL US.

SO WHAT ARE YOU SAYING??

WE'RE SUPPOSED TO DO THE SAME TO HIM?

HE'D **DESERVE** IT.

HOW CAN YOU SAY THAT? WE CAN'T--WE COULDN'T... DO **THAT!**

STOP.

THIS IS STUPID.

HE'S BEEN THROUGH A CAR CRASH AND...

...WHAT I DID TO HIM. THAT'S ENOUGH.

THERE'S NO WAY HE'LL BE ABLE TO FOLLOW US, SO WE'RE JUST GOING TO LEAVE HIM HERE.

WITH AGENT RAMIREZ...GONE... I JUST DON'T WANT TO HURT ANYONE ELSE.

WE'RE NOT **THOSE KINDS** OF **MONSTERS,** RIGHT?

...

OKAY... THE R-ROAD SHOULD BE J-JUST UP AHEAD.

S-S-SEE! I KNEW WE'D FIND THE R-ROAD EVENTUALLY!

GOOD JOB, NEWT!

G-GOD, IT'S COLD. DID ANYONE BRING A B-BLANKET OR SOMETHING?

CHATTER

HEH.

W-W-WHAT??

NOTHING, IT'S JUST... YOU WOULD DIE IN NEPAL. THIS IS LIKE... EARLY SPRING THERE.

OH, R-RIGHT, I FORGOT WE'RE T-TRAVELING WITH THE **ABOMINABLE SNOW BOY** HERE--

HIDE!!

WHY CAN'T WE GET A RIDE WITH **THEM?**

snerk

ARE YOU KIDDING ME?? THOSE ARE THE GUYS WHO WERE STALKING THE GATE--

THEY'D DO **EXPERIMENTS** ON US OR SOMETHING!

snort

WHAT IN THE WORLD ARE YOU LAUGHING AT? THEY ALMOST **SAW US!**

I'M SORRY, I CAN'T HELP IT!

WHAT IS SO FUNNY?!

PFFFFT

HEE HEE HEE

THEIR BUMPER STICKER SAID "I'M SQUATCHING YOU"!

HA HA HA HA HA HA HA HA HA HA HA

PFF

HEH.

HA HA HA HA HA HA HA HA

HA HA HA HA HA HA HA HA HA HA HA

I DIDN'T KNOW YOU MADE ANY NOISE!! YOU CAN LAUGH! WOW!

· · · · · · · · ·

HA HA HA HA HA HA HA HA HA HA HA HA HA HA HA HA HA HA

WE ARE IN **DANGER,**

IN THE MIDDLE OF THE **DESERT,** AND YOU'RE **LAUGHING?!**

PFFT

LOOK AT THE **STARS.**

CHAPTER FOUR
HEAT WAVES

CATCH!

SHH! GO GO GO, QUICK!

PHEW

CLICK

I CAN'T BELIEVE WE MADE IT. FOURTEEN MILES IS SO **FAR!!**

WHUMP

HERE, TINY.

DON'T DRINK TOO FAST, OKAY?

MHM.

gulp. gulp.

HEY... ANYONE NEED THE BATHROOM OR CAN I GO?

NAH.

GO FOR IT.

SO...

WHAT ARE WE GOING TO DO NOW?

WE COULD ORDER ROOM SERVICE!

HAHA, YEAH RIGHT.

I AM HUNGRY THOUGH...

WE ALL ARE.

I THINK I SAW SOME **VENDING MACHINES** OUTSIDE...

BUT WE DON'T HAVE ANY **MONEY**.

OH, UH... WHAT, CLARICE?

RUMMAGE

WHERE DID YOU GET THAT?!

$ $ $

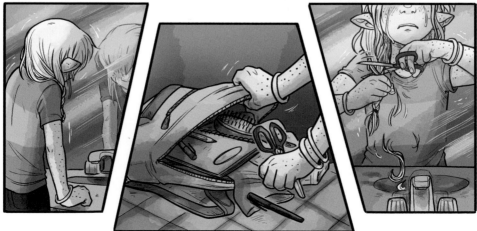

RRUUMBLE

VRRRRRT

RRUUMBLE

GAS

EXCUSE ME, MA'AM, CAN WE ASK YOU A FEW QUESTIONS?

...

...

...

...MISSING KIDS?

NO... I HAVEN'T SEEN ANYTHING.

I'LL BE SURE TO KEEP AN EYE OUT THOUGH.

THANK YOU, MA'AM, WE DO SO APPRECIATE YOUR HELP.

103

WHY CAN'T WE GO TALK TO THE AGENTS? THEY CAN TAKE US BACK TO THE PLAYROOM AND FIGURE ALL OF THIS OUT.

NO. WE CAN'T TRUST THE LOT OF THEM. WE TRUSTED **CLARK**, AND YOU SAW WHAT HE DID.

ANY OF THEM COULD TURN ON US.

I DON'T WANT TO GO BACK TO THE **DESERT**!

WE WON'T GO BACK TO THE DESERT. WE HAVE TO FIND SOMEWHERE ELSE.

YEAH, I SAW A **BUS STATION** TOO.

I DON'T THINK WE HAVE ENOUGH MONEY FOR BUS TICKETS...

...I COULD CALL **MY DAD**.

WHAT CAN YOUR DAD DO?

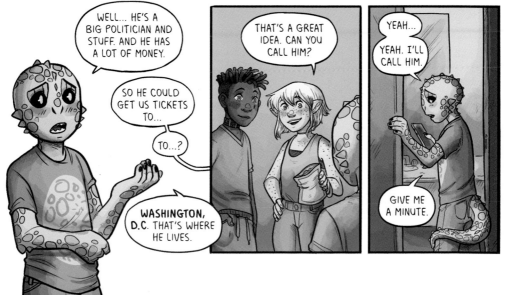

WELL... HE'S A BIG POLITICIAN AND STUFF. AND HE HAS A LOT OF MONEY.

SO HE COULD GET US TICKETS TO...

TO...?

WASHINGTON, D.C. THAT'S WHERE HE LIVES.

THAT'S A GREAT IDEA. CAN YOU CALL HIM?

YEAH... YEAH. I'LL CALL HIM.

GIVE ME A MINUTE.

SOOO...

SYLVIE, I REALLY LIKE YOUR HAIR!

WHY'D YOU CUT IT?

CAN YOU CUT MINE?

OH, UH...

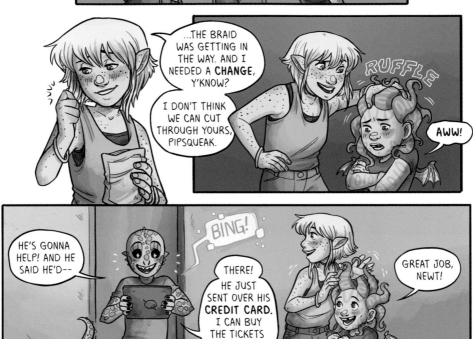

...THE BRAID WAS GETTING IN THE WAY. AND I NEEDED A **CHANGE**, Y'KNOW?

I DON'T THINK WE CAN CUT THROUGH YOURS, PIPSQUEAK.

RUFFLE

AWW!

HE'S GONNA HELP! AND HE SAID HE'D--

BING!

THERE! HE JUST SENT OVER HIS **CREDIT CARD.** I CAN BUY THE TICKETS ONLINE!

GREAT JOB, NEWT!

THERE'S A BUS IN A HALF HOUR...

BUT WE'RE GONNA NEED SOME **DISGUISES.**

THE BUS STATION IS JUST ACROSS THE STREET THERE.

EVERYONE READY?

CLARICE, THE FUR IS A DEAD GIVEAWAY.

fwippy fwip

YOU WON'T NEED TO BE A **SEAL** ON THE **BUS!!**

YANK

CAN'T YOU PUT IT IN YOUR BAG??

HERE--WEAR THIS ON TOP! IT'LL LOOK LIKE A **FUR HOOD**.

VERY FASHIONABLE!

LET'S GO!

SNEAK SNEAK

DASH

THERE'S THE BUS! LET'S GO!

WAIT!

—YOINK—

tp tp tp

HOW ARE WE GONNA GET ON BOARD??

FAKISH

tmp

LOOK! IT'S THOSE SQUATCH GUYS!

CHAPTER FIVE

HIGHLY IRREGULAR

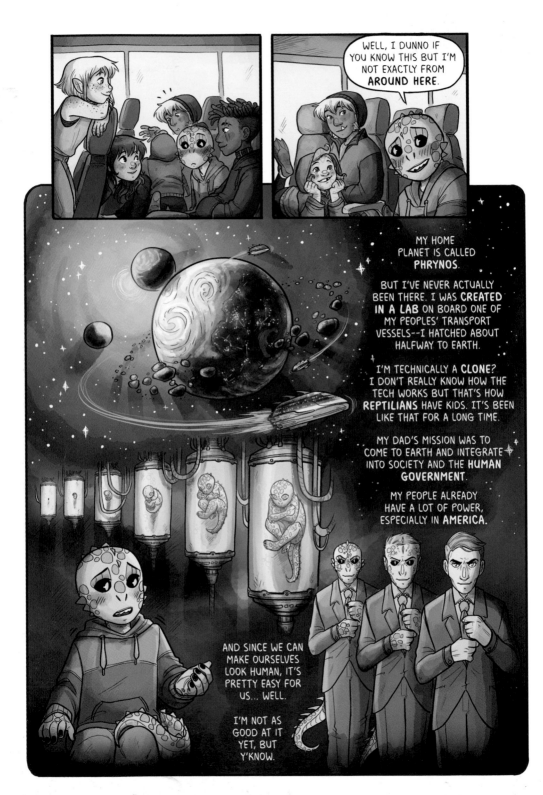

WHEN WE FINALLY GOT TO EARTH, I WAS SO EXCITED!

BUT... I STILL HADN'T MASTERED MY HUMAN FORM.

IT DIDN'T FEEL RIGHT... LIKE IT WASN'T REALLY **ME**.

DAD GOT HIS JOB RIGHT AWAY AND WAS IMPRESSING EVERYBODY, BUT I WASN'T ALLOWED TO LEAVE THE HOUSE.

ALL I WANTED TO DO WAS FIT IN.

SO ONE DAY...

WHOA! COOL COSTUME!

OH, THANKS!

WANT TO PLAY MONSTERS WITH US?

YEAH!

THIS WAY.
KEEP UP.

CONFERENCE
ROOM 1

GREETINGS,
NEWTON.

...HI,
DAD.

123

THERE WAS A BREACH OF SECURITY AT THE PLAYROOM. ONE OF THE AGENTS DOUBLE-CROSSED THEM.

WE STARTED GETTING **THREATENING MESSAGES** AND **BREAK-INS** TO OUR ROOMS, SO THE OTHER AGENTS THOUGHT THEY SHOULD MOVE US FOR SAFETY.

BUT THE DOUBLE-AGENT, **AGENT CLARK,** ENDED UP DRIVING OUR TRANSPORT...

THERE WAS AN INCIDENT AND ANOTHER AGENT WAS... KILLED. **SYLVIE** SAVED US ALL BY FORCING AGENT CLARK TO CRASH THE CAR, AND WE WALKED THROUGH THE DESERT TO FIND A BUS TO...

TO BRING US TO **YOU.**

WAS AGENT CLARK WORKING ALONE?

I'M NOT SURE...

IN THE CAR, HE SAID HE HAD TO TAKE US OR **HE** WOULD KILL HIM.

WE DON'T KNOW WHO "HE" IS.

WERE YOU FOLLOWED?

I DON'T THINK SO. THE BUS WAS **EMPTY** THE WHOLE RIDE HERE.

IT SOUNDS LIKE YOU HAVE BEEN THROUGH QUITE THE ORDEAL.

TYPICAL **HUMANS**.

MISHANDLING **DELICATE MATTERS** SEEMS TO BE ONE OF THEIR **SPECIALITIES**.

I JUST KNEW SOMETHING LIKE THIS WOULD HAPPEN.

THOSE **FOOLS** RUNNING THE PLAYROOM NEVER HAD PROPER SECURITY TO BEGIN WITH.

HOW COULD THEY HANDLE SUCH A COMPLICATED ISSUE?

NO MATTER. I KEPT UP **MY END** OF THE **BARGAIN**.

IT IS NO FAULT OF MINE IF THEY COULD NOT KEEP THEIRS.

B...BARGAIN?

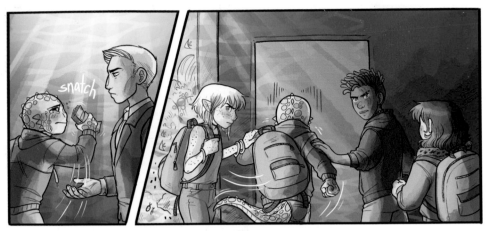

snatch

TIME TO GO, MAGGIE.

OKAY.

fwip

BYE!

STOMP STOMP P

...NEWT?

I'M SO SORRY.

I'M SO SORRY I DRAGGED YOU INTO THIS--AND NOW WE HAVE **NOWHERE TO GO!**

IT'S OKAY, WE'LL FIGURE SOMETHING OUT.

CHAPTER SIX

TWO
HOUSES

TIBBS, DEAR, INTRODUCE ME TO YOUR FRIENDS.

IS THAT A TALKING CAT?!

AH, YES, MY APOLOGIES.

IS THIS MORE COMFORTABLE FOR YOU?

IT'S... A BIT BETTER, YES.

EVERYONE, THIS IS CAT SITH.

THE CAT SITH??

LIKE FROM THE FAIRY TALES??

THE VERY SAME. DON'T BE ALARMED, IT'S NOT OFTEN I'M HOST TO A WISP.

BUT REST ASSURED, YOU ARE SAFE HERE AS MY GUESTS.

SO... WHAT BRINGS YOU TO OUR HUMBLE ABODE?

WE'VE... BEEN TRAVELING FOR A WHILE. WE JUST ARRIVED IN D.C. TODAY.

OUR ORIGINAL PLAN... DIDN'T WORK OUT, AND WE HAVE NO PLACE TO STAY. TIBBS FOUND US BY ACCIDENT--

THOSE F.R.E.A.K.I.S.H. GUYS HAD US PINNED IN AN ALLEYWAY.

OH, THOSE IDIOTS. I DIDN'T REALIZE THEY WERE BACK IN TOWN.

YOU KNOW OF THEM?

SURE DO.

flop

THEY'RE A GROUP OF **CONSPIRACY THEORISTS** WHO'VE GOTTEN A BIT TOO CLOSE FOR COMFORT TO OUR VARIOUS COMMUNITIES. WE'VE LED THEM ON MORE WILD-GOOSE CHASES THAN I WANT TO REMEMBER. THEY'RE NOT **DANGEROUS**, JUST **UTTERLY ANNOYING**.

LAST I HEARD THEY WERE HEADED FOR NEVADA. SOMETHING ABOUT **ALIENS** AND **AREA 51**.

glance

COUGH

DON'T WORRY, YOU'RE SAFE FROM THEM HERE.

YOU'RE WELCOME TO STAY THE NIGHT, BUT IN RETURN I HAVE A **FAVOR** TO ASK.

AS I'M SURE YOU'VE GATHERED, THESE ARE THE **MALKINS**.

BUT WE'RE NOT ALONE IN THIS CITY. UNFORTUNATELY, WE OFTEN CLASH WITH A GROUP THAT CALLS THEMSELVES THE **JACKALS**.

AS PETTY AS OUR SQUABBLES HAVE BEEN, THE JACKALS RECENTLY **CROSSED THE LINE**.

THEY ACCUSED US OF **CAPTURING** ONE OF THEIR MEMBERS.

AND AS **REVENGE**, THEY'VE TAKEN ONE OF OURS. JAYLA.

BUT YOU **DIDN'T** KIDNAP THEIR FRIEND?

OF COURSE NOT!

WHAT REASON WOULD WE HAVE?

BESIDES, OUR METHODS ARE MUCH **QUIETER** AND **MORE SUBTLE**.

IN RETURN FOR ROOM AND BOARD HERE, I WOULD ASK THAT YOU RESCUE OUR MISSING MALKIN.

THE JACKALS KNOW TO WATCH OUT FOR US, BUT THEY WILL NEVER SEE YOU COMING.

TIBBS CAN GIVE YOU MORE INFORMATION AND LEAD YOU TO THE JACKAL HIDEOUT TOMORROW.

THEY KNOW THIS CITY LIKE THE BACK OF THEIR HAND.

FOR TONIGHT, EAT, SLEEP, REST.

THANK YOU, SIR.

THANKS, MR. KITTY!

YOU'RE WELCOME, MY DEAR.

TOSS

CATCH

THANKS!

ISN'T THIS **AMAZING**?? ALL THESE IRREGULARITIES LIVING RIGHT UNDER THE CITY'S NOSE!

IT IS IMPRESSIVE.

munch munch

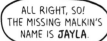

THERE IT IS. WE'VE GOTTA BE CAREFUL NOW, AND NOT LET THEM CATCH US.

THESE DOGS LIKE TO **BITE**.

WHAT?

I MEAN, THEY'RE CALLED THE **JACKALS** FOR A REASON. THEY CAN TURN INTO **WOLVES**.

THIS IS A GANG OF **WEREWOLVES**?!

YEAH, WELL, YOU'RE A **WEREBEAR**, AREN'T YOU? WE'LL BE FINE!

HOW DO WE GET IN?

flap flap

I... DIDN'T THINK THAT FAR AHEAD.

OH, PERFECT.

LOOK AT THE LADDER THINGIES!

OH YEAH, THE **FIRE ESCAPE**! GOOD IDEA, MAGS!

tp tp tp

HOP HOP

rattle

149

DO YOU SEE JAYLA?

NOT YET. KEEP LOOKING!

THAT'S THEIR LEADER, DINAH.

snag

PULL TUG TUG

QUIET!

CLATTER

152

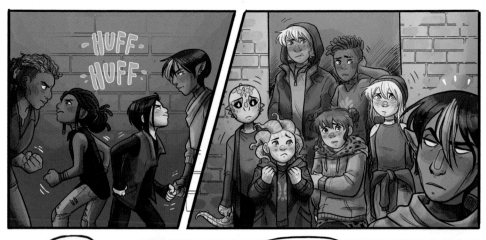

SPEAK THEN.

THIS IS RAY'S.

NEWT WAS ABLE TO UNLOCK IT AND CHECK THROUGH HIS PHOTOS AND MESSAGES.

HE AND JAYLA WERE **TOGETHER**.

WHAT?!

THEY FELL IN LOVE! LOOK AT THEM-- LOOK AT HOW **HAPPY** THEY ARE!

BUT YOU FOUGHT SO MUCH AND WERE SO DIVIDED, THEY KNEW THAT YOU WOULD TRY TO END THEIR RELATIONSHIP.

SO THEY RAN AWAY TOGETHER.

YOU **DROVE** THEM AWAY.

...VERY WELL. FOR THE GOOD OF BOTH OUR HOUSES, WE SHOULD WORK TOWARD **EASING THE TENSION**.

I'LL **PLAY NICE** IF YOU DO, SITH.

I LOOK FORWARD TO... FUTURE... COOPERATION.

...

...DITTO.

WE DID IT!!

I CAN'T BELIEVE THAT **WORKED**!

ARE YOU TWO GONNA BE OKAY HANDLING THIS ALLIANCE?

SEEMS LIKE IT'LL BE TOUGH...

OF **COURSE** WE WILL!

WE'LL KEEP THEM ON THEIR TOES--

MAKE SURE THEY DON'T **KILL** EACH OTHER.

WHAT ARE YOU GOING TO DO NOW?

SITH SAID YOU CAN STAY A WHILE, IF YOU WANT TO.

WE CAN'T REALLY STICK AROUND... NOT WITH F.R.E.A.K.I.S.H. ON OUR HEELS.

WE WOULDN'T WANT TO RISK EXPOSING THE JACKALS OR MALKINS.

MAYBE YOU CAN FOLLOW BEHIND RAY AND JAYLA? FIND THAT SANCTUARY THEY WERE TALKING ABOUT?

THAT'S WHAT WE WERE THINKING TOO.

HERE, TAKE RAY'S PHONE.

ONCE YOU GET THERE, TELL HIM TO CALL ME, FOR HEAVEN'S SAKE.

-SNIFF-
THANK YOU ALL SO MUCH!

I'M GLAD I TRIED TO PICKPOCKET YOUR BODYGUARD.

I TOLD YOU! HE WASN'T MY BODYGUARD--

163

CHAPTER SEVEN

CROSS COUNTRY

SO I KNOW IT'S IN WASHINGTON STATE-- THAT'S WHERE RAY AND JAYLA WERE HEADED.

THEY HAVE A COUPLE OF MESSAGES BACK AND FORTH ABOUT BUS TICKETS AND STUFF...

BUT NO **ADDRESSES**.

CAN'T YOU JUST... LIKE... **GOOGLE** IT?

OH **SURE**, JUST SEARCH "HI, WHERE CAN A GROUP OF SIX **MONSTERS** THAT MAY OR MAY NOT INCLUDE...

A BEAR, A SELKIE, A YETI, AN ALIEN, A WILL-O-THE-WISP, AND **WHATEVER MAGGIE IS**, GO HIDE BECAUSE THE **GOVERNMENT** IS AFTER THEM?"

I'M SURE THAT WOULD WORK OUT **PERFECTLY**.

172

BUH HUH

I MISS MY **ROOM!**

SOB!

I MISS THE **POOL!** AND I-- I--

THIS ISN'T ABOUT THE **STUFFIE,** IS IT?

-SNRK-

AND WE--CRASHED THE **C-CAR** AND NOW--SOB-- WE MISSED THE **BUS**--AND IT'S ALL MY **F-F-FAULT** AND I JUST I'M SO--SO--SO-- **SCARED!**

WE CAN'T STICK AROUND. THOSE **F.R.E.A.K.I.S.H.** GUYS MIGHT SHOW UP BEFORE ANOTHER BUS DOES.

WAAHHAAA..BUH HUH.. HUH HUH...

WE'RE GONNA HAVE TO **WALK** NOW.

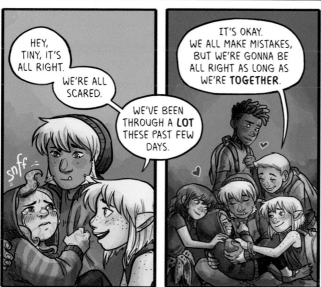

HEY, TINY, IT'S ALL RIGHT.

WE'RE ALL SCARED.

WE'VE BEEN THROUGH A **LOT** THESE PAST FEW DAYS.

snff

IT'S OKAY. WE ALL MAKE MISTAKES, BUT WE'RE GONNA BE ALL RIGHT AS LONG AS WE'RE **TOGETHER.**

WELL... MIGHT AS WELL GET MOVING.

COME ON.

-sniffle-

IT'S A **STATUE!!**

SOMEONE PROBABLY PUT IT UP AS A JOKE.

LOOK, IT'S **POINTING!**

MAYBE THAT'S THE WAY TO A TOWN?

I BET IT IS!

THAT THING SCARED THE CRAP OUT OF ME.

ME TOO!

ME THREE.

PHEW

MIGHT AS WELL FOLLOW ITS DIRECTIONS. FIND SOMEPLACE TO CHARGE YOUR O-PAD, NEWT.

YEAH.

LET'S GO!

BUS 3 MILES

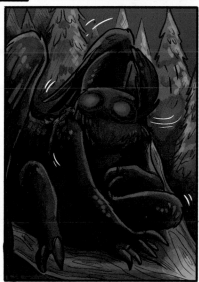

WHAT'S THAT LIGHT UP AHEAD?

LOOK! THERE'S THE BUS STATION!!

UGH

OH, THANK GOODNESS--

THERE'S **POWER** AND **WIFI** HERE.

tap tap

YAAAAWN

CRACK

WHEN'S THE NEXT BUS TO SEATTLE?

WELL... WE DON'T EVEN KNOW **WHERE** THE SANCTUARY IS... OTHER THAN WASHINGTON STATE.

WASHINGTON CAN'T BE *THAT* BIG, RIGHT?

SORRY, MAGGIE, WASHINGTON IS **VERY** BIG.

SO HOW DO WE FIGURE OUT WHERE THIS PLACE IS?

CAN'T WE JUST ASK FOR **DIRECTIONS**?

WHO WOULD WE EVEN ASK, TINY?

WHAT DO YOU MEAN, CLARICE?

...US?

WE DON'T KNOW WHERE IT IS, CLARICE. THAT'S THE **PROBLEM**.

OH! **OTHER** IRREGULARITIES!

RAY AND JAYLA HAD TO LEARN ABOUT IT FROM *SOMEONE*, RIGHT?

SO WE JUST HAVE TO FIND SOME MORE CREATURES LIKE US TO ASK!

BUT HOW ARE WE GONNA FIND THEM?

STUMBLE ON THEM IN THE MIDDLE OF THE NIGHT AGAIN?

nod nod

HANG ON A SECOND!

tap tappa   *tap tap*

THE SQUATCH GUYS **MAPPED IT OUT** FOR US ALREADY!

OH YEAH!

FRESNO NIGHTCRAWLERS
Fresno, CA

Only seen through pixelated film, these Ghost Pants are thought to be alien life-forms.

LOOK!

WHAT IF THEY REALLY HAVE IRREGULARITIES HERE?

MUSEUM OF CRYPTIDS

LIVE SPECIMENS

IT WOULD BE A PERFECT **COVER STORY**, HONESTLY.

Believe or DON'T

LET'S CHECK IT OUT!

WHY ARE THEY ALL **NAKED??**

WHY ARE WHO ALL WHA--

HEY!

I THINK... I THINK I'M OFFENDED.

YUCK!

IS THAT REALLY A **NANDI** BEAR?

JAALI?

NO, **I'M** A NANDI BEAR. THAT'S JUST... **A** BEAR.

A **SICK** AND **OLD** BEAR WHO SHOULDN'T BE **IN A CAGE!**

snff snff

whuff

CLANG

I'M SORRY.

THAT WAS... A BAD SHOW.

YEAH.

GIFT SHOP

EXIT

ARE YOU OKAY?

SNIFF

BUT THAT DAY...

RAAAAAARRGHH!!!

IT'S THEM!

ssssshhffff

BLAM!

BAM

BAM

BAM

mwwhuuff?!

195

CHAPTER EIGHT

BRIEF RESPITE

UH... THANKS FOR THE RIDE.

AIN'T NO PROBLEM--WHAT WERE Y'ALL DOIN' OUT HERE ANYWAY??

UHHH... WALKING?

HAH, WELL, I GATHERED THAT MUCH! BUT WALKIN' WHERE?

AH... I SEE.

NO PLACE TO GO, HUH?

WHY DON'T Y'ALL COME HOME WITH ME? **IRREGULARITIES** SUCH AS YOURSELVES WILL **FIT RIGHT IN.**

I CAN SPOT Y'ALL A MILE AWAY, SEEIN' AS I'M **MARRIED** TO ONE.

HOW DID YOU--??

SINCE YOU GOT NO PLACE ELSE TO GO, MIGHT AS WELL COME TO OUR HOUSE.

I'M SURE MY FAMILY WOULD LOVE TO MEET'CHA.

OR AT LEAST MY WIFE CAN GET Y'ALL SOME DRY CLOTHES AND A HOT MEAL.

WHAD'YA SAY?

SIR...

NO OFFENSE, BUT WE DON'T EVEN KNOW WHO YOU ARE.

202

THEY ARE... AND I'VE BEEN THINKING ABOUT THEIR OFFER. THIS COULD BE **HOME,** SYLVIE.

YOU KNOW WE CAN'T DO THAT.

WHY NOT? IT'S PRIVATE AND PEACEFUL HERE, AND THE FAMILY IS WONDERFUL.

IT'S SO GOOD TO SEE MAGGIE PLAYING WITH KIDS HER OWN AGE. WHY NOT JUST **STAY?**

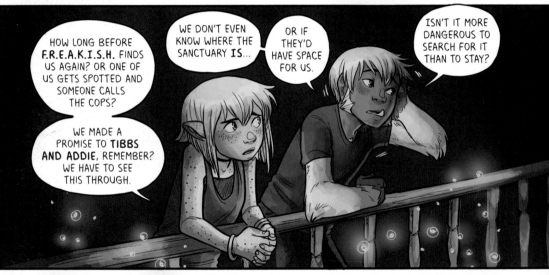

HOW LONG BEFORE **F.R.E.A.K.I.S.H.** FINDS US AGAIN? OR ONE OF US GETS SPOTTED AND SOMEONE CALLS THE COPS?

WE DON'T EVEN KNOW WHERE THE SANCTUARY **IS...**

OR IF THEY'D HAVE SPACE FOR US.

ISN'T IT MORE DANGEROUS TO SEARCH FOR IT THAN TO STAY?

WE MADE A PROMISE TO **TIBBS AND ADDIE,** REMEMBER? WE HAVE TO SEE THIS THROUGH.

I JUST WANT US ALL TO BE SAFE.

I CARE **SO MUCH** ABOUT THEM, EVEN IF I'M BAD AT SHOWING IT.

AND I WANT TO FIND A PLACE WHERE WE **BELONG.**

IF WE GO AND CAN'T FIND IT, WE CAN ALWAYS COME BACK HERE.

215

KNOCK KNOCK!

WHO THE--

IT'S SO **LATE!**

BE CAREFUL, CARIÑO.

CAN I HELP YOU?

GREETINGS. WE ARE THE FRATERNITY OF RESEARCHERS TO THE EXISTENCE OF ALL KNOWN INTELLIGENT SUPERNATURAL HUMANOIDS.

WELL, THAT'S A MOUTHFUL.

ALSO KNOWN AS F.R.E.A.K.I.S.H.

WE HAVE REASON TO BELIEVE THERE MAY BE SEVERAL **CRYPTIDS** NEARBY. HAVE YOU NOTICED ANY STRANGE ACTIVITY?

HOW DID THEY FIND US *AGAIN??*

GASP!

YOU'VE GOT THIS.

nod nod

SPLASH

YANK

221

226

CHAPTER NINE

UNRAVELING

GUH! I'M SICK OF WEARING ALL THIS **STUFF**!

IT'S **HOT** AND IT SQUISHES MY **WINGS**!

fumble

WE'VE TALKED ABOUT THIS--NORMAL PEOPLE WOULD **FREAK OUT** IF THEY SAW YOU.

I HAVE TO DO MY HUMAN FACE AND HIDE MY TAIL. WE ALL HAVE TO LOOK HUMAN.

BUT THAT ONE GUY THOUGHT I WAS WEARING A **COSTUME**!

BING-BONG

I KNOW BUT HE DIDN'T GET A VERY GOOD LOOK AT YOU. WE JUST DON'T WANT TO GET IN TROUBLE OR SENT BACK TO THE PLAYROOM.

SWIP

SWIP

ONCE WE'RE IN THE SANCTUARY I'M SURE YOU'LL NEVER HAVE TO WEAR IT AGAIN.

...FINE.

I MISS ALEX'S COOKING SO MUCH.

I'M TIRED OF **FROZEN BURRITOS**.

YEAH, ME TOO... LET'S HOPE THIS PLACE HAS SOME **REAL** FOOD.

HOP HOP HOP

HNNNNNNG!

fwip

WHAT ARE WE SUPPOSED TO DO, DOYLE? JUST **LET THEM GO**??

WE'VE ALREADY CALLED THEM IN-- THAT COLLECTOR GUY IS **EXPECTING** US!

WE'VE BEEN PAID, WE'VE FOLLOWED THEM ACROSS THE COUNTRY!

WE'RE SUPPOSED TO BE CRYPTOZOOLOGISTS, NOT **KIDNAPPERS**.

UHH... WE'RE **KIDS**, YOU'VE **NAPPED US**. BY DEFINITION YOU'RE **DEFINITELY** KIDNAPPERS.

AND YOU TOOK OUR **SNACKS!** WHAT'S THE POINT OF BEING KIDNAPPED IF WE CAN'T HAVE ANY **SNACKS?!**

KNOCK KNOCK

LET'S PUT IT TO A VOTE. WHO WANTS TO TURN THEM IN?

o o o

YEAH... I THOUGHT SO.

THEY'RE JUST KIDS, MAN. MONSTER KIDS, BUT KIDS...

HEY... WE WANNA TALK.

snatch

ARE YOU GONNA **LET US GO**??

LISTEN, SORRY ABOUT ALL THIS... WE'RE JUST TRYING TO DO WHAT WE WERE **PAID** FOR.

WHO WOULD PAY YOU TO **STALK AND KIDNAP** A BUNCH OF **KIDS**?!

WE DIDN'T **KNOW** YOU WERE KIDS!! WE JUST THOUGHT... I DUNNO. YOU WERE SOME KIND OF **INTELLIGENT HUMANOIDS**? WHICH, UH, YOU **ARE**! I MEAN, YOU'RE **WAY** MORE HUMAN THAN WE THOUGHT YOU'D BE?? OR IS THAT **INSULTING**? CRAP--

CRONCH

WAY TO GO, BEN.

...SORRY.

WE KNEW YOU'D HAVE TO BE **INTELLIGENT**, OBVIOUSLY. YOU COULD USE OUR **TECHNOLOGY**.

WHAT DO YOU MEAN?

WE TRACKED YOU BY **TRIANGULATING** THE SIGNAL FROM AN **O-PAD**.

NOT TO SOUND EVEN MORE LIKE A BUNCH OF STALKERS, BUT WEREN'T THERE SUPPOSED TO BE **SIX** OF YOU?

DOES IT **MATTER??** ARE YOU LETTING US GO OR **NOT?**

WE'RE DEFINITELY LETTING YOU GO. I HAVE A MILLION QUESTIONS TO ASK A REAL LIVE **YETI, REPTILIAN,** AND...

OCTOPUS... GIRL?

BUT... YEAH.

WE JUST HAVE TO FIGURE OUT WHAT TO TELL THE COLLECTOR.

THE **COLLECTOR?!**

WELL... YEAH, HE'S THE ONE WHO HIRED US.

WE DON'T KNOW MUCH ABOUT HIM, BUT HIS ESTATE IS A LITTLE NORTH OF HERE.

WE'RE SUPPOSED TO BRING YOU TO HIM. HE'S A COLLECTOR, WE FIGURED HE'S GOT LOTS OF CRYPTIDS.

PLUS HE... --AHEM-- PAID IN **CASH.**

OMAR, OH MY GOD--

IT'S A TRAP.

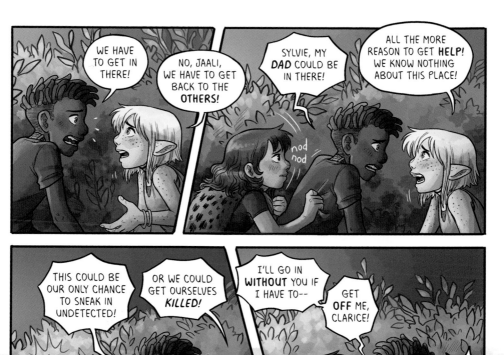

LET ME GET THIS STRAIGHT.

YOU'VE BEEN ON THE RUN FOR WEEKS BECAUSE YOU ESCAPED **AREA 51**--

CONTAINMENT 9, ACTUALLY, BUT YEAH, IT'S THE SAME THING.

AND YOU HEARD ABOUT THIS SANCTUARY FOR IRREGULARITIES, BUT IT TURNS OUT IT'S A **TRAP**...

...SET BY THE COLLECTOR--**OUR BOSS**--WHO IS ACTUALLY CAPTURING CREATURES LIKE YOU AGAINST THEIR WILL??

AND NOW OUR FRIENDS ARE IN DANGER. THEY LEFT TO SCOUT OUT THE ESTATE.

WHAT THE--?

THAT'S MY O-PAD!

BING!

OH.. UH, RIGHT, SORRY.

OH NO...

IT MIGHT ALREADY BE **TOO LATE!**

HELKP; TRAP WERR CAGUHT HFELP

CHAPTER TEN

HOME

AGHH HHH

CLARICE??

JAALI?

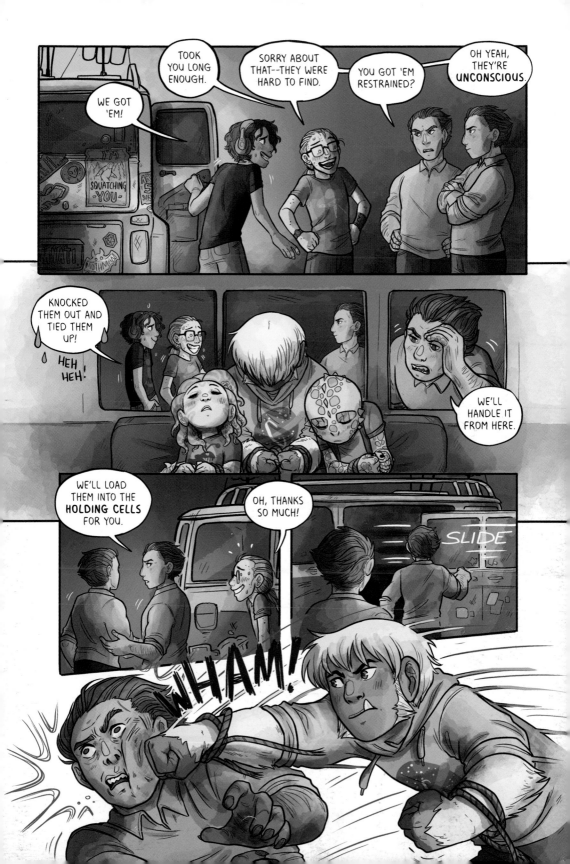

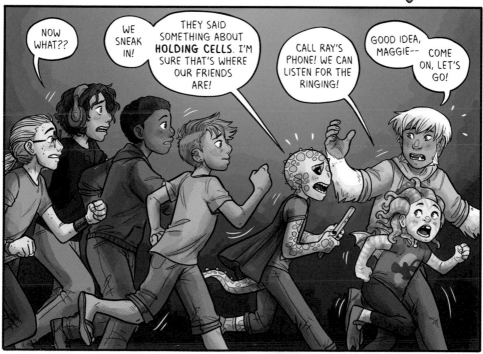

HEY!

LET ME OUT. I HAVE MY ANSWER!

SYLVIE??

WHAT DO YOU WANT?

TAKE ME TO THE COLLECTOR. I'M READY TO **JOIN HIM.**

WHAT?!

TRAITOR!!

AFTER ALL THIS TIME.

WE--WE'RE **FAMILY!!**

HOW COULD YOU **DO** THIS?!

HOW DID YOU GUYS GET IN??

WE HAD SOME HELP FROM OUR NEW FRIENDS.

HIIII...

EH HEH...

IT'S THE SQUATCH GUYS!!

IT'S OKAY! THEY'RE OUR FRIENDS NOW!

SORRY ABOUT THE WHOLE... STALKING... THING...

WAIT, WHERE'S SYLVIE?

SHE'S BETRAYED US.

SHE LEFT TO JOIN THE COLLECTOR.

DAD!!!

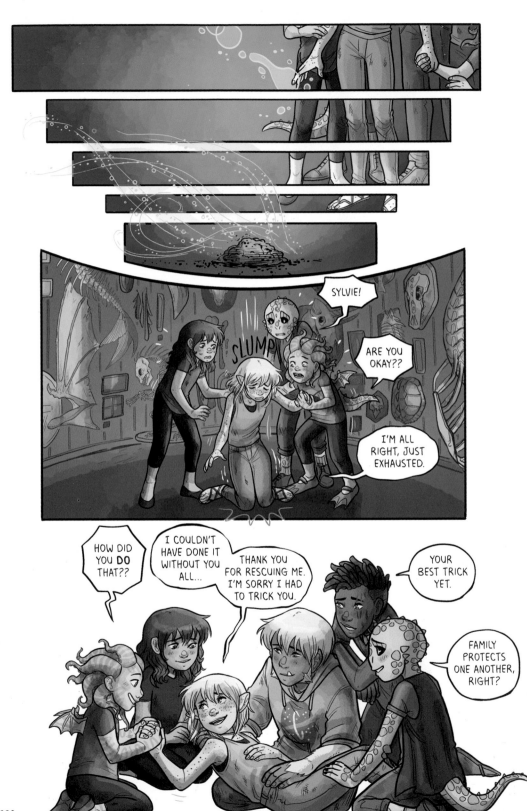

282

I FOUND YOUR BANGLES, SYLVIE.

I DON'T THINK I'LL BE NEEDING THOSE ANYMORE. WHY DON'T YOU WEAR 'EM FOR ME?

WOW, REALLY??

YOU **SAVED** US. I KNEW YOU WOULD.

I THOUGHT I WAS GOING TO LOSE CONTROL...

YOU? **NEVER.**

SHUT UP, YOU DUMMY.

Y'KNOW... THIS PLACE IS REALLY BEAUTIFUL WHEN IT'S NOT A **SHADOW MONSTER'S HUNTING GROUNDS.**

WHAT ARE WE GONNA DO NOW?

THE COLLECTOR'S GONE... WHAT IF WE MADE A *REAL* SANCTUARY?

MAYBE **THIS** COULD BE OUR HOME.

I LIKE THE SOUND OF THAT.

I DON'T CARE **WHERE** HOME IS...

HOW DOES NEWT DEAL WITH **THE TAIL**?

buttons

opening

HIDDEN SEAM PANTS!

flap

THE VERY FIRST DRAWINGS OF THE MAIN CHARACTERS.

THIS IS RETCH! ONE OF THE ORIGINAL CONCEPT CHARACTERS, BUT HE DIDN'T MAKE IT TO THE FINAL VERSION.

ANOTHER KIND

ANOTHER KIND

ANOTHER KIND

COVER SKETCHES

ANOTHER KIND

ACKNOWLEDGMENTS

THANK YOU TO OUR FRIENDS AND FAMILY FOR THEIR UNENDING
SUPPORT AND ENTHUSIASM THROUGHOUT THE CREATION OF THIS BOOK.
YOU KEPT US GOING AND INSPIRED SO MANY OF THE FAMILIES IN THIS STORY.
WE LOVE YOU!

THANK YOU A MILLION TIMES OVER TO SAVANNA AND GIGI—OUR UNBELIEVABLY
AMAZING FLATTERS WHO MADE THIS BOOK POSSIBLE THROUGH THEIR
PATIENCE, PERSEVERENCE, AND DEDICATION TO THE MEME. BDB FOREVER.

THANK YOU TO CLAIRE, THE AGENT OF OUR DREAMS, WHO GEEKED WITH US THE
WHOLE TIME AND IS MAGGIE'S #1 FAN IN THE ENTIRE UNIVERSE. THANK YOU
FOR HELPING US MAKE THIS HAPPEN.

THANK YOU TO ROSE, ANDREW, AND JOE AT HARPER FOR BEING
THE BEST TEAM WE COULD ASK FOR! Y'ALL ARE CHAMPIONS AND WE
CAN'T WAIT FOR THE NEXT.

THANK YOU TO OUR HOME OFFICE FURRY COWORKERS FOR ALWAYS
LAYING ON US WHEN WE WERE TRYING TO GET WORK DONE.
MANY SCRITCHES AND PETS FOR YOU.

SHOUT-OUTS TO THE DIPPERS—OUR FIRST AND BIGGEST FANS. THANK YOU
JOAN HILTY, ALEX FINE, THE ELDRITCH CREW, THE GIRL* GANG,
THE PEPPER PAUPERS, LOREN COLEMAN, AND THE CRYPTOZOOLOGY MUSEUM.
THANK YOU TO *BUZZFEED UNSOLVED*, *THE ADVENTURE ZONE*, *CRITICAL ROLE*,
AND WAY TOO MANY PODCASTS FOR HELPING KEEP OUR MINDS OCCUPIED
THROUGH THE TOUGH TIMES.

TO ALL THE CRYPTOZOOLOGISTS WHO
HAVE COME BEFORE US. WITHOUT YOUR
DEDICATION TO THE STUDY OF WEIRD
PHENOMENA, WE MIGHT NEVER HAVE
LEARNED TO LOVE THEM JUST LIKE YOU DO.

AND FINALLY—
THANK YOU FOR READING!

FOR DOYLE
AND FOR OUR FAMILIES,
OF ONE KIND OR
ANOTHER